What If EVERYBODY Said That?

Words by **Ellen Javernick** **two lions** Pictures by **Colleen Madden**

Published by Two Lions, New York

www.apub.com

Amazon, the Amazon logo, and Two Lions are
trademarks of Amazon.com, Inc., or its affiliates.

ISBN-13: 9781503948952 (hardcover)
ISBN-10: 1503948951 (hardcover)

The illustrations are rendered in mixed media.
Book design by AndWorld Design

Printed in China
First Edition

10 9 8 7 6 5 4 3 2 1

To my grandchildren:
Ally, Katy, Haley, Carly,
Ty, Izzy, Zack, Nina,
Cedar, and Meg.
—E. J.

For Mr. Key.
The King of Kindness.
—C. M.

At the park some kids asked if they could play with me. I said, "No boys allowed."

NO BOYS

Their mom yelled at me, **"What if EVERYBODY said that?"**

In art class we were drawing dogs.
I looked at the other kids' pictures
and said,

"Those don't look like dogs to me,"
and I laughed.

The art teacher made me apologize.
"What if EVERYBODY said that?"

At the beach, I just wanted to scare my cousin. "Look!" I teased. "THERE'S A SHARK!" The lifeguard heard her screaming and called down to me,

"What if EVERYBODY said that?"

SHHARRRKKK!!
SWIMMING POLAR BEAR!
MONSTER HERMIT CRABS!!
AAAHH!
Peanut butter and Jelly fish!!
The under toads!

During sharing time at school, I really wanted to tell my class about my new shoes. I shouted, "ME FIRST! ME FIRST!"

Our teacher frowned at me and said,
"What if EVERYBODY said that?"

When a boy in my class got glasses, I said, "You sure look FUNNY!"

The principal heard me. He shook his head.

"What if EVERYBODY said that?"

When one of the kids forgot her lunch for our field trip, the guide asked some of us to share ours. I said, "NO WAY! I'm going to eat mine all by myself."

The guide glared down at me.
"What if EVERYBODY said that?"

When our teacher was in the hospital, the substitute suggested we make him get-well cards. I said, "Maybe later. I'm busy playing now."

Get Well SOON

ow.
oww!
YEE owww!

The sub held up the empty card box.
"What if EVERYBODY said that?"

On the soccer field, when my team was losing, I said, "This game is dumb. I QUIT!"

The coach blew her whistle.
"What if EVERYBODY said that?"

When a new kid moved
in next door, I told her,
"I've got plenty of
friends already,"
and I didn't invite
her to play.

Mom heard and gave me a disappointed look.

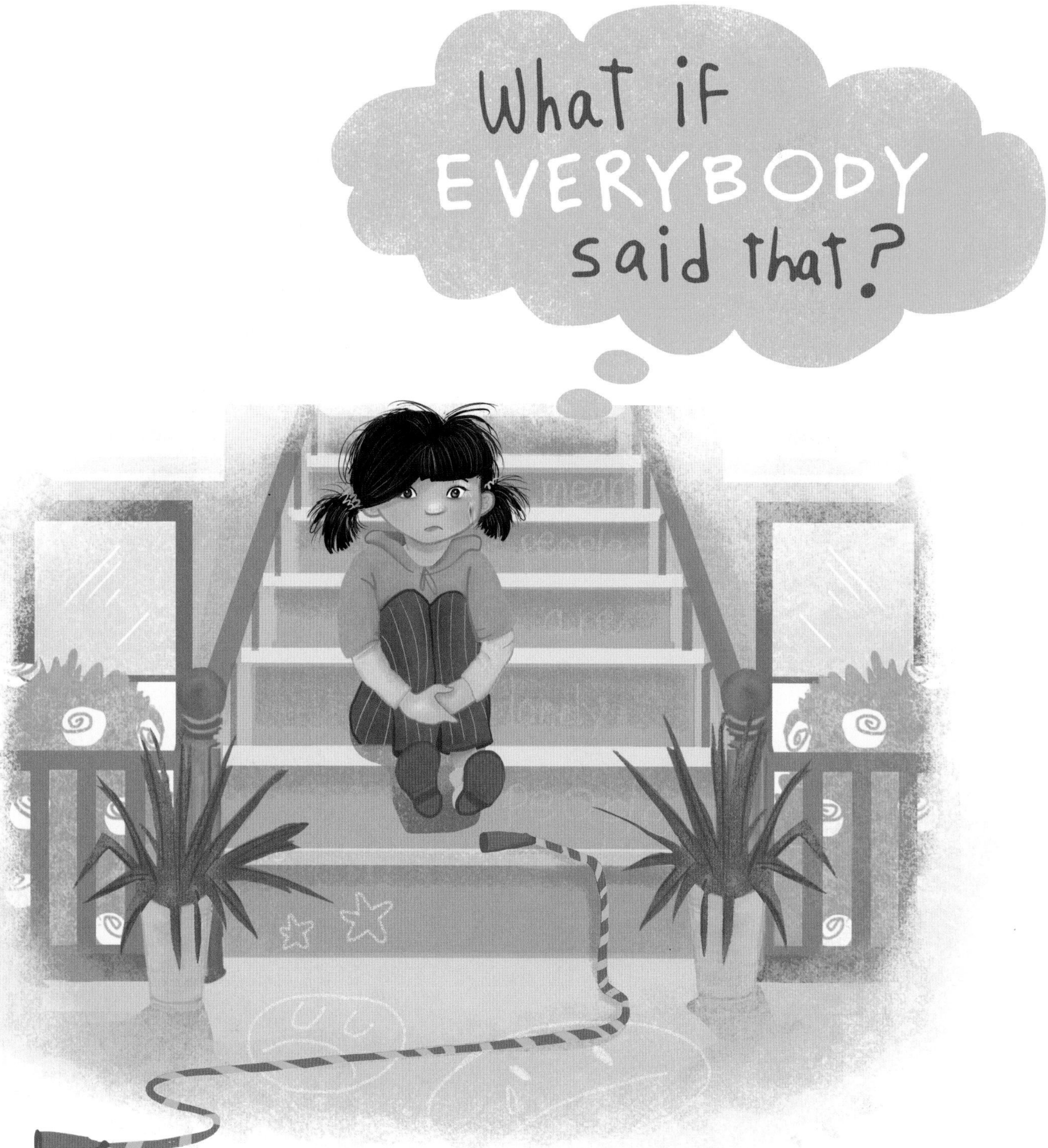
What if EVERYBODY said that?

The next day I went to the girl's house.
I said to her, "I'm sorry. Let's be friends."

What if everybody said THAT?

EVERYBODY SHOULD!